CC  ꜱꞭ ᴖꞤꞮꞮꞙ

…Stories to travel by

"Short tales about African-American men, their actions and reactions to everyday situations."

COMMUTER SHORT STORIES

…Stories to travel by

"Short tales about African-American men, their actions and reactions to everyday situations."

By

ARTHUR P. MCMAHAN, Ph.D.

1stBooks - rev. 4/4/00

About The Book

A book of contemporary short stories about everyday people in everyday situations who are confronted with the decision to help others or to ignore calls for help. The stories are written in a familiar tone that is both humorous and thought provoking. Issues facing African-Americans are addressed in a careful but light manner so that readers can make their own value judgements. It's easy reading designed for commuters who want something short and interesting to read as they commute to and from work or just want to relax with a good short story.

Acknowledgements

Thanks to the following individuals for their part in making this project possible:

NeAnni Ife for the poem in Eulogy of A Homeless Man.

Carla Foggie for the cover design and all of the professionals who assisted in the typing and lay-out.

Dedication

I dedicate this book to my parents Mary and Robert McMahan. I give them all of the credit for any success that I've experienced in my life. To my teachers at Cumming Street School in Spartanburg, S.C. who played a tremendous role in my development. My parents, family, teachers and my belief in God have all contributed to my deep concern and compassion for my fellow man.

CONTENTS

EULOGY OF A HOMELESS MAN

Introduction

As he sat on the hard, weather beaten bench softened by stacks of smelly clothes and news papers, he looked out over his unfortunate domain and wondered how he'd ended up here. The bench was this man's home. It was bordered in the front by a small area of filthy concrete stained mostly by human urine and pigeon waste. Three feet away to the rear was Republic Boulevard, a busy through street where cars, trucks and buses scurried along twenty-four hours a day as people made their way to and from their home. Although it's difficult to imagine someone becoming overly excited about living on a park bench, it was actually quite a feat for him to acquire this prime real estate in a time and a place where space for the city's homeless was becoming more and more scarce. Many of his homeless colleagues were actually sleeping on sidewalks and over grates. Unless fate slapped him with a kind spin for a change, this corner, this bench would be his last known residence.

Thomas Jones moved his shopping cart full of rags, blankets and other stuff from one of the shelters to this new spot about two weeks ago. He really wanted to make the shelter experience work, because it was safer than living on the street. Despite his concern for safety there was too much going on inside the shelter that he could not tolerate. There was drug usage, thefts and other mischief. Above all though, he couldn't stand the humiliation of waiting in line, night after night in hopes of getting a cot to sleep on. Yes, he was homeless, but even homeless people have principles. He knew that if anyone deserved to sleep in the shelter he certainly did because he was truly a homeless person. Thomas had a very hard time understanding why a person who didn't really have to live on the streets would choose to do so. It was the most degrading experience he could think of.

It was early morning and Thomas had to pee. He never considered what an imposition it was to eliminate body waste until he became homeless. He drank a couple of beers last night and his bladder was full. At the last minute he arose slowly from the bench, moved to the edge of the grass near a five foot hedge bush, pulled out his private from his already open fly and urinated. This routine was not unusual for Thomas, this was his spot, this was where he lived, slept, ate and used the bathroom. He often wondered if tourist and others knew why downtown areas reek of the smell of human waste? He answered rhetorically, "it's because stores, shops, restaurants and office buildings downtown have banned homeless people from entering and using the restroom, and when you've got to go, you've got to go!"

Suddenly, emerging from within the bush flapping his wings, vigorously shaking off the warm yellow urine that was raining on him was a gray common pigeon. The slender gray pigeon with a touch of neon green around his neck and black bands around his bony legs just above the feet was outraged that someone had urinated on him. Pigeon pee was one thing but he could not stand the smell of human pee. The pigeon hovering in mid-air like a helicopter, shouted in a very irritated tone:

Hey! What the hell do you think you are doing? Thomas could not speak, he was in shock. He was pretty sure that he would poop in his pants. He thought to himself, the alcohol, the drugs, the depression, the anger, all had finally pushed him over the edge. He was not only homeless, he was crazy!

Dammit man, I said what the hell are you doing?

Thomas, voice trembling, hand still holding his private finally spoke. I had to take a leak and you were in my damn bathroom!

What do you mean your bathroom? I have been sleeping in that bush for a week. That is my house man! the bird said angrily.

Listen you pissy little bird. First of all, I must be crazy to talk to you, secondly, you'd better calm down or I'll kick your little bird butt, and put you on the grill! Thomas coughed that horrible hacking cough of a life long smoker, with a wheeze in between coughs. He spat out a bunch of phlegm that was red with blood as he completed his tirade.

The threat of being barbecued and the sight of that awful phlegm that shot from the homeless man's mouth caused the pigeon to gather himself and apologize:

Okay, Okay, I'm sorry. Maybe I over-reacted. But, have you ever had anyone piss on your head?

Quite frankly said the homeless man, I have. Once I slept over a grate with a card board box covering me. Some kids walking through the city stopped and took a whiz on my box. So yes, I have been pissed on. So to summarized my fine feathered friend, I'd much rather be pisssed off than pissed on.

Well, I guess since we're neighbors we should introduce ourselves.

Okay! Who the hell are you, other than a bite sized talking chicken sandwich?

Nice to meet you too! I'm Peter, Peter the Pigeon, and you?

I'm Thomas Jones. Nice to meet you. Why don't you come on over to the living room and have a seat? Thomas made his way slowly back to the bench, his shoulders slumped, his clothing ragged and dirty, his mind cluttered. Extended exposure, walking and sleeping in rain, snow, hot weather, and cold weather had weakened him and allowed disease to fester in his body, The deep hacking cough was symptomatic of the severity of the disease. Peter walked over to the bench, he only flew when absolutely necessary. He perched on the seat beside Thomas. They were quite the pair. A broken homeless man and a pigeon sitting on a wooden bench staring at one another trying to figure each other out. Neither of the two had anywhere else to go, neither had any thing better to do.

So Pete?

Don't call me Pete jack-ass! You humans are always shortening names. My name is Peter, Peter the frigging pigeon.

Okay, okay, Peter, da the Pigeon. What are you doing down here on the ground? Shouldn't you be with the other birds flying high or living on the roof of some skyscraper or something?

Not exactly, my homeless brother, I should be living in our natural habitat where trees, grass, berries and other plants are plentiful for food and shelter. You think pigeons have always lived in the city, walking these dirty streets begging for bread crumbs from you humans? No, no, no. We are a proud group, with a great heritage who once occupied a great wilderness that is now your city.

Wait a minute mister pigeon. Are you saying that if it was not for the unfortunate circumstances cast on your people by my people, you wouldn't be hanging out downtown begging for bread and pooping on people's head and on their cars?

That's exactly what I'm saying Mr. Thomas. Thirty years ago, this was all wide open space. My family lived on a farm where we raised our children, worked and cared for each other. Our primary profession as you know is flying. I am a pilot just like my father before me and his father before him. Well, one day out of nowhere came the bulldozers. They flattened Mr. Foster's farm where we lived, it took only ten minutes to destroy all that he'd lived and worked for all of his life. But more importantly, all that the pigeons had, our home, our neighborhood, our friends, everything was wiped out. Then came the buildings. First, there was one, then five, then ten. Soon the entire area was covered with brick and glass skyscrapers.

So what happened to you and your pigeon people?

We had no choice. We moved into the lofts and onto the roofs of the buildings. But the problem was, there was no food up there! So we had to come down to the streets. We began searching the trash bins and any other place we thought there'd be food. You know, I really fell in love with those McDonald's french fries! So we'd eat and then return to our nests high on top of the buildings.... The pigeon was interrupted by the nagging, hacking cough with the intermittent wheeze of Mr. Jones.

Excuse me Peter.

Your cough seems to be getting worse. Don't you think you should go to a doctor and have it checked out?

Yeah. He chuckled, but no doctor will see me. I have no money and no insurance.

But Mr. Thomas, I'm really worried about you. That cough seems serious.

Ha, Ha. You're worried about me. You and your pigeon people were pushed from your natural habitat and forced to live in the city where you have no food, no family, no friends. Then, when you finally find a bush to live in, some homeless bum, takes a leak on you. No, no, I'm worried about you, Peter.

You know, we were just about to become used to our new homes on top of the skyscrapers when things began to change. The new building technologies and the poisons used by the building maintenance people ran us away from the tops of the buildings. We were forced down to the streets with you. That's why whenever you come to the city, you see pigeons walking around on the streets hunting and pecking for any small morsel of food they can find. We have no fear of humans because like all animals, once you have looked destiny in the face and discovered that there is no future, there is nothing else to fear.

Thomas Jones, teary eyed and coughing, and otherwise feeling like shit, looked at Peter and said, I'm sorry. I am sorry for all of us. I thought my life was hard.

What could possibly be so bad for a human? You guys have big brains to think, long legs with feet to walk and run, and you basically are in charge of the entire planet. Humans have houses, cars, airplanes, etc. By the way Mr. Thomas, where is your house?

My house*?* What do you mean you bird brain? You are sitting your pigeon ass in my house as we speak. *(*the angry outburst made him cough, he coughed and hacked for more than a minute). I'm sorry Peter, we humans do have a lot of advantages over you and other animals. But unfortunately, things don't always work out for us individually. While most humans are fortunate enough to have a house and other essentials, some of us are homeless. This bench we are sitting on, is my house for now.

Peter flapped his wings once and rose to the top of the back of the bench. He lifted one wing as if to point and say, *you mean all of this is yours?* **He chuckled to himself.**

9

Mr. Thomas was obviously distressed that a pigeon could make fun of him. He sat still for a minute, angry with himself for getting angry with a pigeon. As the conversation resumed, a well dressed couple walked briskly past the man and the pigeon. The woman whispered to her companion, "honey, I swear that pigeon and that man were having a conversation!" The male responded, "oh sure, there are a lot of strange things going on in the city, but if that pigeon can talk, then I can fly." Peter the pigeon, winked at the woman as she turned her head for one last glance. They hurried past.

Peter laughed hysterically, between the curious pedestrians and this, this homeless human who thinks this park bench is his home, he thought he'd laugh himself to death.

Thomas Jones was forty-seven or forty-eight. He really didn't remember. He looked like a beaten and broken sixty-five year old. As he sat and listened to the pigeon ridiculing him, his heart sank and he began to sob. He sobbed and coughed, coughed then sobbed. He was feeling the pain of the journey that brought him to this point in his life. He said to the bird while staring at the ground: "if you knew how I was feeling about the way my life turned out, you probably wouldn't laugh so hard."

Mr. Thomas, I'm really not laughing at you. I am still tickled from a fantastic direct hit today. I mean, I dropped a load that splattered the top and the windshield of the prettiest little red BMW you have ever seen. The pigeon then said in a more subdued tone: *you know, you homeless humans and us pigeons have a lot in common. It seems as if today, we are fighting for the same food crumbs to eat, the same city parks to sit and to sleep, and the same filthy streets from which we beg for mercy.*

Perhaps, we do have some things in common Mr. Pigeon, but I'm a man. I should be doing better. As a matter of fact, I was doing a lot better. I have not been homeless all my life.

What happened Thomas?

It's a long story Peter. I'm sure you have better things to do than to listen to my sad song. I'm just an unlucky soul, who, because two or three calls didn't go my way, ended up homeless, and penniless on these streets. I don't blame anyone, it's not anyone's fault but mine. But I tell you Peter, if just one of the calls had gone my way, one event had happened differently, perhaps I wouldn't be sitting here today talking to a pigeon on a park bench.

Thomas, I don't believe any of us pigeons or people would choose to end up homeless on the street if we had other options.

Yeah, but when you listen to news reports, read the paper, or listen to the people walking the streets, homelessness is the result of lazy, no good, drug addicted bums who just don't try hard enough.

So what is it Thomas, is there a list or sequence of events or occurrences that usually lead to homelessness?

Like I said before Peter, for me it was just a string of unfortunate events that forced me into becoming homeless. (Thomas coughed and gagged for about two minutes. He appeared to stop breathing at one point during this episode). I lived with the most wonderful wife and children in the world. I worked in a manufacturing plant in Alabama for fifteen years. We had a very nice home. We paid our bills and went to church on Sunday. We were a happy family. Now looking back, I can identify the point where things began to change.

Things were going very well in the plant where I worked. Because of my tenure and work record, I was promoted to supervisor. The plant was making lots of money and we worked sometimes 20 to 30 hours of overtime per pay period.

My wife and I decided to buy a new and bigger house because things were going so well. Six months after I purchased our new home, the company opened a new plant in Mexico. It wasn't long before we began to feel the effect of the new plant's impact on production. The supervisors were the first group to be downsized. Because I was recently promoted, I was the easiest to fire. It was a nightmare. Before I realized what hit me, I was an unemployed, 40 year old man with a new house, and a wife and kids to support. I can't tell you Peter, and I don't know if anyone could possibly understand how small I felt at that moment. In one instant I went from a production wage earner to an unemployed man with an uncertain future.

Damn, that's bad. To quote one of my feathered friends, "that's buzzard's luck."

Well, that was just the beginning. But Peter, please understand that thousands of people who are now homeless were once productive, upstanding citizens but one catastrophic event pushed them over the edge. Look at it this way, most of the homeless that you see, once had homes or someplace to live.

So what you're saying is, as we judge the homeless, we should consider that many are not there because of their lack of effort. Some are mere victims of circumstance.

I tried my best Peter. I begged for work, but I could not find a decent job. I began going down to the corner where the men gathered for day work. Trucks would come by and pick a group up to perform labor for the day and drop them off in the evening. Most of the men drank to help make it through the day. It wasn't long before I picked up the habit.

I bet that didn't go over too well with your wife.

After the bills began to pile up, and we began to argue and fight over the smallest things, finally she took the children and left. (As Thomas spoke, he slumped down on the bench and sobbed). That, Mr. Pigeon was the saddest day in my life. (Thomas cried and coughed while thinking of his wife and children. He tried not to think of them because it always made him feel miserable).

So that's the way you get rid of a wife? Peter said with a chuckle. Hoping to lighten things up a little.

You know bird brain, that's really not funny, Thomas said matter-of-factly. However, it is important to note that people you think care for you will drop you like a hot potato if you fall on hard times. I didn't see or hear from any of my family or friends after my wife left.

13

What did you do once you lost your family?

I bummed around, drank, did day jobs when I could find them, and I slept wherever I could. One day while wandering through the streets and not eating for four days, I saw this cook throw chicken into a trash bin inside the store. I walked in smelly, dirty, and hungry and went into the bin and promptly picked out the chicken and began to eat. The next thing I knew, I was being arrested for trespassing and theft.

Speaking of mans inhumanity to man! They arrested you for eating the food that had been thrown way? Pigeons would never treat other pigeons that way. If a pigeon is hungry and needs food, other pigeons will see to it that he eats.

The social values that we preach and teach require us to help those in need. But in reality, the practice of how we treat the needy is quite different. In our society, we will arrest and prosecute an individual more harshly for stealing food than for committing other more serious crimes. Don't get me wrong, stealing is a serious crime, but a starving animal must be fed, for if not, he become vicious. (Thomas appeared to be weakening).

So Thom, you went to jail because you removed chicken from a waste can in order to eat?

Well Peter, I didn't exactly go to jail. After I was cited for stealing, I left town in order to avoid going to jail. That's how I happened to come to the city. I was a stowaway on a train and this hobo advised me to go to the city, he said you could almost make a living begging for money.

Thomas, I know I have a small brain, but how do you figure man will give you money when you ask for it, but will arrest you for eating food from a trash bin? That just doesn't seem logical!

A desperate man is often open to the most frivolous suggestions, and I was and am a desperate man. I just needed some glimmer of hope and the city provided that. But right now, my hope is fading Peter. I've given it all I have. I tried to live my life the right way, but look where its gotten me. On a frigging park bench with no food, no shelter, no hope, and talking to a damn pigeon. (Thomas breaks down and the strain of his cough forces him back on the bench. His glazed tear filled eyes are barely open, and he can't find the pigeon). Peter, (he mutters), Please come down so I can see you.

4

Peter flaps once and lands on Thomas' chest with a look of concern and pity. He is regretting that he'd spoken so harshly to this obviously broken man. Peter asked Thomas, *where will you go from here? Can I get you some water or something to eat?*

Thomas smiled with his eyes closed. No one had been nice to him or offered to help him in a very long time. No thanks Peter, he whispered. Your presence here with me is worth much more than food or water.

Peter, sitting on Thomas' chest, looked into the homeless man's eyes. He thought of how desperate he felt when he first came to the city. He thought of all the homeless men and women he'd seen on the street during his time in the city and how he never took the time to try to understand what circumstances led to their condition. *Thomas,* he said, *you've done well. You worked hard and tried to play the game. Life threw you two or three curve balls in a row and you were called out. But you my friend, are not a failure. You are a victim of circumstance. Where are your human brothers to pick you up in your time of need? How can you humans boast of your superiority over all animals when you won't even feed a hungry man? This reminds me of the question I read in one of your good books: "Is it nothing to all ye who passeth by?" When they pass a homeless person standing, sitting or lying in the streets, does it inspire any emotion, or do they simply tense up, make sure they avoid any eye contact and move quickly on their way?* (As Peter was in the middle of his oratory, a nicely dressed man approached the two. He could not figure which was more bizarre, the site of a homeless man lying on his back with a pigeon sitting on his chest, or the thought that the pigeon appeared to be conversing with the man?) The man avoided eye contact and quickly moved on his way. Peter wondered how the man would have reacted if Thomas had been bleeding. He quickly answered his own question, humans just don't give a damn about homeless people. If a man who appears to be homeless is lying in the middle of the sidewalk, chances are no one will stop to see what's wrong. *Thomas, there is something that's just not right about this behavior. As a pigeon, I must say that I am appalled that man, the keeper of the earth, caretaker of all things great and small, do not practice what he preaches.*

By now, Thomas was almost unconscious. The lack of food, proper medical attention and the demoralizing effect of living on the street had worn him down. He was giving up. He was prepared to turn his soul over to the great protector. Thomas said to Peter, there is one thing I would like for you to do for me:

What is it? I'll do anything that I can!

Thomas reached into his coat pocket and pulled out a yellowed, stained piece of paper with words scribbled upon it. *Please read this to me and then see to it that it gets to the newspaper after I'm gone.*

Peter was feeling very somber. He'd never seen a man die, but he knew that Thomas' demise was inevitable. He took the piece of paper with his beak and spread it out flat against Thomas' chest, holding it down with his feet. Peter could feel the sensation of Thomas' weakening heartbeat through the paper and through his feet. Tears welled up in Peter's eyes as he began to read:

Eulogy of a Homeless Man

As I approached you on the street and politely asked you for something to eat. You looked right through me with your cold, icy stare and acted as if I were invisible . You walked right past me. You were ill at ease, but you have nothing to fear. I am not a disease that you catch from looking at or speaking to me. Beneath the dirt and the rags is a man you don't see. I was a homeless man. You rushed past me everyday on your way to work with your brief cases filled with papers and contracts; on your way to the mall with your wallets filled with cash and credit cards; on your way from reality with your brains filled with misconceptions and prejudice. I suppose you thought that by diverting your eyes from me, I would disappear. You know — out of sight, out of mind. Well, it's not quite that simple. I am here. We are here. And it doesn't look like we'll be going anywhere any time soon. Not all of us are crazed junkies, out to terrorize everybody who crosses our paths. Not all of us are rejects from some overpopulated, under-funded mental health facility. Some of us were once just like you. We had homes. We had families. We had jobs and dignity and self respect. But we lost it, all of it. We could deal with the loss of home and job. We could deal with the loss of status and money. But when a man is stripped of his dignity and self respect, he loses everything. And generally, his family is the first thing he loses. From that point on, little else matters. I say this, not because I expect sympathy or even want it, but because I seek understanding: not for me. It's far too late for that, but for the others, especially the young ones. They still have a chance. When you look at them, see them as human beings. See the bags they carry, the garbage bags of life, filled with adversity and turmoil. Don't ignore them. If they ask you for something that you don't want to give, say "No," but please, don' t ignore them. Acknowledge them as you would any other stranger on the street. Look, I know you're afraid of them; afraid they'll attack you, afraid they'll spit on you, afraid they'll get to close to you.

And I know that's not all you're afraid of. I know what your real fear is, even if you're unwilling or unable to admit it. We are men and women, once filled with hopes and plans, but sometimes our fate is just out of our hands. Sometimes the fire just burns out too fast and we find that our problems are simply too vast, and they become way too much for us to bear. So we give up on life. We just do not care. The things that once mattered don't matter anymore and life becomes too much of a chore. We find ourselves chasing dreams that never come true and we believe that giving up is the only thing left to do. We grow tired of our hopes being knocked out by despair. I leave this life without a song or a tear. You could be where I am. And that is your fear.

5

Thomas's life expired sometime during the reading of his eulogy. His battle was over at last, his status restored. He wouldn't have to live on the streets anymore. He wouldn't have to beg for food, long for his lost family, or ponder over why all of these things happened to him.

Peter sat as still as Thomas' heartbeat for a few minutes. He contemplated his brief but rich experience with this human who had no home. He was appalled at man's inhumanity to each other. Peter saw similarities in what happened to pigeons (and other animals) and what happens to some humans. Peter thought how ironic it is that pigeons and homeless people share the same meager existence on the streets of the big cities and small towns. Both are seen as a nuisance that people would rather do without. Each was forced to move from their valued habitat into an area where there is a significant reduction in the quality of life. Like the pigeon, the homeless man is often blamed for his own demise. Peter learned from Thomas that it is not always a lack of effort or talent, but rather a series of unfortunate events that propels a man into homelessness. Peter was astonished that people could or would not make eye contact with their homeless brothers. Yes, he knew that part of the reason was to avoid being asked for money, but there had to be more. He surmised that man was reluctant to look into the eyes of his down trodden brothers because of what he might see. Somewhere deep in the eyes of the homeless person is a mirror that will perhaps reflect an image of the viewer that is uncomfortable and hard to deal with. This image, perhaps, shows man as an insensitive self centered soul, lacking the capacity to reach out to others who are in dire straits. Then again, maybe man is simply afraid that his life, his own little cocoon, will be upset if he stops to help another. Maybe man is afraid of what happens to him when he demonstrates compassion to others. Or maybe man simply feels helpless when it comes to the homeless.

Peter thought what a waste. People like his friend Thomas

who have so much to offer, are written off as useless losers. If only there was some way that Peter, a lowly pigeon, could help man to understand that to be homeless does not mean to be without dignity. It does not mean to be without sensitivity. It does not mean to be without desire. And most of all it does not mean to be without hope for overcoming this condition.

Thomas Jones died today without fanfare, without any close friends or family by his side.

The lesson he taught me during our short friendship is that every man, regardless of condition deserves to be looked in the eye. Each of you are important and have something to contribute. When you fall, you deserve to be picked up.

Each precious moment spent by one man helping another who is in need, will re-supply the diminishing pool of humanity that once seemed so plentiful.

Peter wondered who would discover Thomas' body, who would ensure his proper burial? Would anyone attempt to contact his estranged family? He flew down from Thomas Jones' cooling body and walked away as a gust of wind blew the self-styled eulogy into the street.

The end

Epilogue

It's not clear to scholars or soothsayers whether Peter the Pigeon actually walked and talked with Thomas Jones on the day in question but what is abundantly clear is that a homeless man died an undignified death. His heart, his hopes and dreams expired a long time ago. Fortunately for him and perhaps for us his death ended his misery.

Each day hundreds, perhaps thousands, of men women and children pass on unnoticed by a society that prides itself on its moral fortitude. Today the clock struck twelve for Thomas Jones at the corner of Republic Boulevard and the only witness was a slender gray pigeon with a touch of neon green around his neck and black bands around his bony legs just above the feet.

His name was Peter.

AMEN

METRO-MAN

1

*"Yea, though I walk through the valley of the shadow of death,
I will fear no evil; for you art with me; your rod and you staff
they comfort me." (Ps 23:4)*

Alexander Rogers wandered aimlessly through the streets of the capital city for what seemed to him like weeks. He experienced the crime, drugs and other afflictions of the inner-city life. In actuality it had been four nights and five days since he walked away from all that he had ever hoped and dreamed of: a family, a nice home with fancy cars and few worries. One day after his release from City hospital, still physically weak and emotionally drained from his accident he left everything behind in search of the meaning of life!

Alexander felt weak and nauseous. He was hungry for food and starving for sleep, neither, of which he had much of in the past four days. The smoke from burning tires and the stench from years of piled up trash made him feel as if he would throw up all of his internal organs and then, die. When he departed his home without money, change of clothes or his favorite car, he had no idea that his body and mind would be in its current state after such a short time. He swore off all of the material things that had dominated his life to this point. His heart hurt because he had to leave his family. But his journey was not by choice; he was driven by a force greater than him. He needed to find a way to make sense out of his existence. There had to be something he could do to help. Most of all he knew he had to help Jimmy Lee and other manboys, who were the coupe-de grace that started his transformation.

Alexander walked continuously stopping only when he had to relieve himself or when accosted by a fellow street person or policeman. He was even robbed once. The robber left in disgust because Alexander had absolutely nothing of value. He had nothing of real value. Alexander kept walking and thinking, thinking and walking. He was dirty and unshaven. As he peered ahead he could tell that the alley ended abruptly and a grove of trees began. Alexander walked down the steep hill and sensed that he crossed an imaginary line that separated the chaotic city from the quiet serenity of nature. Dazed and confused Alexander Rogers wandered into the woods, paused, and took a deep breath. His lungs could feel the difference in the quality of the air although he was only a couple of hundred yards removed from city. As he peered upward through the tops of the magnificent trees he wondered how things could have gotten so bad for him. The serenity and peacefulness of the forest is what he hoped his new life would be.

Heavily burdened from his dilemma and physically weak from his accident Alexander flopped down onto a gigantic tree trunk lying perpendicular across a small stream. With his eyes closed he gently rubbed his dirty hands across the tree bark, marveling at the beauty and preciseness of nature. With the warm sun cascading downward through the treetops onto his aching body Alexander felt a surge of energy. The energy helped to clear his clogged mind and he acknowledged, to himself, the magnitude of the challenge he faced.

While tears blackened by the dirt on his face, streamed down into his mouth, Alexander spoke aloud for the first time in days. "God," he asked, "what can I do? Why have you brought me to this place?" Alexander was both horrified and humbled by his reference to God. Although raised in a God fearing home where he attended church regularly, Alexander hadn't thought of God in quite some time. He abandoned all of his religious affiliations when he left home for college. He deduced that a career in the business world was not compatible with that "old time religion." Despite his total abandonment of his religious beliefs, he found himself in his greatest time of need, calling on God. Alexander began to feel that something special was happening to him, as he sat in an oasis at the edge of an urban hell, trying to get a handle on his life.

Without warning and without conscious effort Alexander spun himself around and landed on his knees in front of the tree. He plucked a wild berry from a nearby bush and cupped it in his hand. The words came back as clear as his ABC's: "this is my body…. Do this in remembrance of me." He ate the berry. In a trance like state he then reached his hand into the small stream and scooped a handful of the cool refreshing water that tricked through the woods near his makeshift alter. Again, he recalled the words: This is my blood… Do this in remembrance of me. After he had drank the water he began to pray. "God, I have stumbled to you today because there is no where else to turn. There are millions of young men in our country, who are lost or have gone astray, both in a moral and legal sense. I call them manboys. They have no structure that will properly shape them and no moral compass to guide them. Please give me the strength and courage to stand up and to help…"

The prayer continued for over forty minutes. Before Alexander wrapped up his prayer, he had fallen asleep. He lay with his head against his tree his feet stretched out to the edge of the stream. Alexander dreamt of the accident that had brought him to this point and back to God.

2

"Cast all your anxiety on Him, because He cares for you."
(1 Peter 5:7)

The last thing he remembered was a bright flash of brilliant white light that illuminated the downtown Metro Center. The hot yellow glare was as bright as the light above a patient on an operating table as he drifts into oblivion after the anesthesia is administered. Alexander Rogers could not discern the source or the direction of the light. He knew nothing at this moment. Following the flash was a moment of intense calm, the greatest feeling of peace that he could ever recall. Alexander Rogers felt that he was on a clear plateau that was neither here nor there. His plate was clean and his mind clear. Perhaps the time had come to meet the Maker. Perhaps the time had come to answer the question: What have you done to help somebody? Alexander Rogers did not know what happened, he did not know where he was, he knew nothing, he was unconscious. He lay sprawled on the edge of the platform with one leg and one arm hanging over the side.

A fellow traveler, a tall lanky fellow dressed in a five-button suit, carrying a snake skin brief case, flipped open his cell phone to call 911. A soldier with ribbons and buttons from his belt buckle to his collar, rushed over to help control the rapidly forming crowd of curious onlookers. A smallish woman of Asian decent identified herself as a nurse and immediately began to clear the blood and administer CPR to this sharply dressed black professional who appeared to be in critical condition.

One minute passed, two, three minutes. What seemed as if it were an eternity to the startled witnesses was in fact a relatively short five minutes wait for uniformed paramedics who briskly made their way onto the scene. Two huge individuals in white uniforms, who together looked as if they weighed at least a ton, rushed to the victim and quickly began administering aid.

The metro cop, yawning and straightening his uniform,

slowly meandered to the scene to find a bloodied faced, black man in his mid thirties bleeding profusely about the face, and from all indications, who appeared to be unconscious. The metro cop watched as the Asian female and the two paramedics attended to the victim. The officer often wondered if all of the rushing and pushing, running and shoving that occurs during the rush hour would one day lead to some type of bizarre confrontation between man and machine. This incident at first look appeared to fit his idea of a bizarre confrontation. The officer thought of himself as a pretty wise fellow, although others would argue to the contrary, but he just couldn't figure why seemingly intelligent people would storm through a metro station at a hundred miles an hour when there was always another train approaching within minutes. After questioning several eyewitnesses, the Metro cop deduced that the individual in question had run smack into the train as the doors were closing.

3

"Rest in the Lord, and wait patiently for Him." (Ps 37:7)

Alexander Rogers lay in a bed of soft pink rose petals that provided the softest most aromatic bed he could imagine. He felt as if he was in a cocoon that provided the calming sensation of being in a womb.

The last thing he heard was that annoying synthesized voice saying "doors closing, doors closing, and then the light! A devastating, hot, white flash that exploded on the scene as if the comet Hale-Bop had descended to give us non-believers a better view of her newest passengers.

He began to think back on his childhood. Alex, as friends referred to him, grew up in Nashville with his mother, father, and two sisters. His mother was a schoolteacher and his father a brick mason. His father was a Vietnam War hero who suffered periods of drug abuse and depression. The drug addition caused turmoil and despair in the household occasionally but they remained a tight family in spite of it all. Mom and Dad demanded excellence of Alexander and his siblings.

They lived in a very modest three-bedroom house his dad built shortly after he began his contracting business. It was a well-furnished house filled with plenty of athletic equipment because the entire family enjoyed sports. Alexander was a very good athlete. He was successful in all sports, especially baseball and basketball. Alexander Sr. pressed Junior to compete hard and to always be prepared. He insisted that he practice and study, study and practice. His intent was to assure that his son would be stronger and wiser than he had been. Dad knew that preparation would put him in a position to take advantage of opportunities that often can be about because of hard work and dedication. So, regardless of the sport Alexander prepared himself by diligently conditioning his body through long distance running, calisthenics, and weight lifting. Alexander Rogers understood what motivated his father to push him so hard. He did not rebel against his father's sometimes over-bearing enthusiasm. He accepted the notion he had to succeed for this generation as well as for those who came before.

Alexander Rogers Sr. pushed his son harder than the cowhands of the old west pushed their cattle! He pushed Junior to make up for his shortcomings. He felt that he, his dad, and his dad before him should have accomplished more with their lives and he was determined that Junior would not suffer the same failure.

Alexander Sr. was drafted out of high school to fight in the Vietnam War. He never quite understood who or why he was fighting. The terrible things that he saw and experienced during the war and the confusion of the times all were factors in his becoming a heroin addict. He had been a good student in high school with lots of God-given athletic talent. Teachers felt that with a bit of nurturing, and lots more studying, Alexander Rogers could become a doctor, lawyer, teacher, or whatever he wanted. After a Vietnam tour of two years, four months, one day and two hours, Alexander Sr. left the Army and he was never the same again. All of his hopes and dreams were shattered.

One of the stories he often told Junior was about the time when a Vietnamese kid killed all but three of the soldiers in his unit with a hand grenade. This very friendly country guy from Mississippi befriended the boy and invited him into their camp. One day the little boy came back to camp with a package for his friend whom he called "American GI." After the massive explosion there were only three survivors. Alexander was recognized for heroism above and beyond the call of duty when he dragged the two surviving soldiers more than two miles to safety, under hostile fire. This was his favorite recollection of a terrible time in his life.

Alexander married his childhood sweetheart Rose Porter when he returned from the Army. Although he had the intelligence to become a successful professional he chose masonry as his trade. He enjoyed masonry because it allowed him to be creative. It also allowed him the freedom to work independently.   Since the war he had trouble working in structured situations where there was always someone telling him what to do.   He resented authority because he was bitter about having been drafted when there were others who were allowed to escape the draft.

The drive and ambition that Alexander Rogers Sr. once had for himself was willed to his son.   He instilled in Alexander to take pride in himself and study, study, study.   Junior knew dad's entire life story from memory: from the days of growing up outside Nashville, the time he spent in the Army, to the day he was released from the VA rehab center, and all the gory details in between.   He even knew of the illegitimate son Alexander Sr. parented by a woman in GAS Bottom, while deep in a six-month drug stupor.   He often wondered if he had seen the little boy in Gas Bottom who could have been his little brother.

4

"Those who wait for the Lord shall renew their strength, they shall mount up with wings like eagles, they shall run and not be weary,they shall walk and not faint."
(Isa 40:31)

Although theirs was a middle class neighborhood it was just a stones throw from a drug- infested, run down area referred to as Gas Bottom. No one knew where the name originated but it was speculated that the entire area was built on a natural gas leak. It was a desolate place where kids dropped out of school by ninth grade and no one seemed to notice or to care; little boys and little girls spent their developing years hustling, selling drugs, raising themselves, never knowing that life offered something much better than that which they were being forced to accept. Gas Bottom was a barren land that produced little fruit.

Alexander's most vivid memories of Gas Bottom were the times when he would jog through the hood while training for one of his sports teams. While running he could see the sights, hear the sounds and inhale the smells of a place, not far from his own, where hope had died or perhaps, never lived. The houses were three room unpainted, wooden pens with doors falling off the hinges, trash and old appliances strewn across the dirt lawns. Stray dogs and cats wandered about the neighborhood perhaps desperately searching for the animal version of Dr. Jack to take them out of their misery.

On countless occasions while jogging, Alexander came face to face with a puzzling life form he came to call manboy. His definition of the term manboy is a teenager deprived of his childhood and forced to live in the streets like a man. Physiologically he is boy, environmentally he is man. A manboy is a kid who by some cruel fate is destined to live within the confines of a morally and physically decadent area, usually in or around a city. If manboys were born into a different environment, they would not be manboys they would just be boys. Each manboy looks amazingly like the others; a youthful face barely into puberty, baggy, logo-ridden clothing, a backward baseball cap or a scarf, and very large, untied sneakers that cost too much money. The expression on their faces is usually one that says quite clearly "don't mess with me, I'm a manboy and I'm nothing but trouble. My life and my death will be in the streets, do you wanna play?"

What was always most striking to Alexander were the eyes. He had read somewhere that the eyes are the window to the soul. Despite the chronological age of the manboys, they all had muddy eyes that told a terrible story. They were eyes that seemed to bare the weight of all that is wrong and unjust and evil in their world. Eyes that frighten unsuspecting passersby because they feared what the manboy is capable of doing. Alexander was sure that you could transplant a manboy's eyes into a sixty year old who had lived a tough life and no one would know the difference. Strangers fear manboys because the media highlights every bad thing they do. It is the photograph of the manboy that is plastered over TV screens and newspapers everyday in our country.

5

"How beautiful upon the mountains are the feet of the
messenger who announces peace, who brings good news, who
announces salvation, who says to Zion, 'Your God reigns.'"
(Isa 52:7)

For a moment he was completely thoughtless, as if
something had sucked all the matter from his head. His mind
was a clear space, a vacuum. He was sure that someone looking
at him from the front, could see through his head clear to the
other side. He thought to himself, this must be the way it
appears from the inside of an airhead. All he needed at this
point was a small gerbil running around and around on a wheel,
to power his thoughts, and he would be as smart as some
politicians he knew.

Like a stealth periscope rising from a German submarine, a
full-length color image of Jimmy Lee Jenkins slowly rose to fill
the blankness of Alexander's head. The image centered itself
and became his only focus.

The first thing Alexander noticed was his eyes. Eyes that
appeared yellowed with age. Eyes that longed to be cleansed by
the tears of a long, innocent cry. Old eyes delicately set in a
young boy's otherwise immature face. Jimmy Lee Jenkins, a
manboy, was the last face that Alexander Rogers, Jr. wanted to
see. Jimmy Lee was the cause of Alexander's recent bout with
depression. The anxiety he caused was the reason Alex began
questioning himself and his worth. Alexander felt helpless and
inadequate because he didn't know how to reach out and help
Jimmy Lee and other manboys of the world. Jimmy Lee and all
the other manboys of the world were haunting Alexander. Once
a very concerned citizen, Alexander had abandoned his moral
conscience for money and material wealth. The manboys who
monopolized his thoughts were sent to remind him.

Alexander was pushed into a cluttered hallway of the
hospital closest to the metro station where he was hurt. City

hospital was one of only a few places in the area where low-or no-income patients could be treated. It was quite ironic that Alexander, a man of means, had ended up in this hospital for treatment. To his left and to his right were seriously ill patients who would be attended to whenever the intern on duty could get around to it.

Alexander was accompanied to the hospital by Kim Chin the nurse who helped him at the scene of the accident. Nurse Chin while very aware of the rift between blacks and Asians, at least as portrayed in the media, was determined to administer to the sick and the needy and she did just that without regard to their color or ethnicity. Chin knew that there were those in the Black community who felt threatened by people of Asian decent but were unwilling to sit down and discuss ways to promote the group's co-existence. She was an optimist who believed that all could be worked out between Asian Americans and African Americans. For some strange reason she sensed a connection between this stranger, Alexander Rogers, and herself. She knew her way around City Hospital and would see to it that he received the best care possible.

Nurse Chin spotted the doctor on duty, approached him, identified herself, and immediately set about persuading him to examine the metro man right away. Dr. Brockington responded brusquely, "Nurse, I will get to him as soon as I attend to this gunshot victim. You see the 14 year old in the bed over there? He was shot five times in a drive by and his chances of reaching fifteen are rapidly diminishing." Rogers did not hear the conversation, but he would have understood, another manboy fulfilling the prophecy.

Alexander Rogers, Metro Man, was indeed a special guy just as Nurse Chin had suspected. He was a fairly good looking six-foot three individual with a medium build. He was clean shaven, with a closely cropped hair cut that could have caused him to be mistaken for a Marine. But Alexander was no Marine. He was a bright, articulate young man with a pleasant personality and a cordial disposition until a couple of years ago when he began to change. As he began to blend more into the corporate culture, he felt his consciousness, his desire to help people, his deep concern for social justice, slowly slipping away.

When Alexander graduated from high school in 1979, he wanted to move as far away from Nashville Tennessee as possible. Nashville, with its small town mentality, limited social and economic opportunities was definitely not the place he wanted to make his fortune and raise his family. He knew deep inside that he had to leave Nashville because he hated Gas Bottom. But even then, he knew he would never escape the menacing sights of the manboys that he first discovered in Gas Bottom. He knew that he and the manboys with their haunting eyes were connected. He just did not know how, or more importantly, why.

During his first year at Georgetown, Alexander decided that if he was going to make the world a better place for others, it would be in the area of economic development. He chose Economics as his major and Finance as his minor. The years of training for sports had instilled a keen sense of discipline and Alexander excelled as a student. Not only was he an exceptionally accomplished student, Alexander Jr. was socially conscientious too.

Alfre Summers was an academic scholar from Washington. From the time she was a little girl she knew she wanted to be a teacher. Although it is not as fashionable to become a teacher these days, her commitment to helping children convinced her that teaching was her calling. Alfre and Alexander fell in love and were married in June after their graduation from Georgetown. She loved Alexander as much for his deep social conscious as she did for his charm and his intellect. They were sure that they would be in love forever, and that together they could really get things done. Bianca, their first child was born in 1987. Alexander knew that he would push her as hard as his father had pushed him.

Alexander's acceptance to the Harvard Business School was one of the greatest moments in his family's history, or so it seemed. There was a big party with family, old friends, fraternity brothers, and even an old high school teacher.

41

Alexander Jr. had prepared for this moment all of his life and now things were falling into place. The training and studying, coupled with the consistent prodding by his father propelled him to a position where he could attend one of the finest schools in the world.

~6~

"Fear not, for I am with you, do not be afraid, for I am your God."
(Isa 41:10)

Nurse Chin yelled, "Get Dr. Brockington out here STAT!" The annoying monitor attached to Alexander was silent. There were no beeps, no ups and downs in the electric green line that signified life. Physically he was in big trouble but deep in his sub --conscious he was being baptized. Nurse Chin the calm professional knew that without immediate attention his physical vessel would be terminated and this strangely likable Metro man would be dead!

Alfre rushed into the emergency ward just as they wheeled Alexander's bed through the double doors with a sign that read, Danger - High Voltage! She approached the first person she saw dressed in hospital garb and mouthed hysterically "My husband, my husband! The confused orderly slowly removed his Orioles baseball cap, scratched his head and responded, "Mam, I am not your husband but if you can wait ten minutes till I go on break, we can get married in the hospital chapel." Nurse Chin, noticing this odd exchange, rushed over and introduced herself and asked if Mr. Alexander Rogers was her spouse?

While Alexander lay in limbo, somewhere between life and death the two women began to talk. Nurse Chin spent the next half hour giving Alfre the details of her husband's accident and his current condition. As the conversation evolved, they began discussing the hectic pace of living in the Washington Metropolitan area. They spoke of the contradictions of the way individuals live from one neighborhood to the next and the almost embarrassing level of health care that the poor and unfortunate is forced to accept. The latter being the reason why Kim Chin had dedicated her life to providing health care to the inner city. Chin worked the inner city despite the fact that a larger percentage of her patients were African American. Alfre,

43

the teacher, tried to explain to the nurse that while inner city ethnic groups should work together, it's a natural phenomenon that minority groups competing for similar status within a larger society often find themselves at odds. Inter- ethnic racism and hatred hurts both groups, it brings us all down, she preached. She went on to say that it is incumbent upon individuals within these groups to reach out to each other and to work for the common good, rather than emphasizing differences and building barriers. Nurse Chin and Mrs. Gray were pleased that their communication at that moment could serve as an example of how dialogue is a great way to begin building understanding.

7

"For God so loved the world that he gave his only begotten Son, that he who believeth in him should not perish but have everlasting life." (John 3:16)

As Alexander Rogers lay in the critical care section of the hospital, and as his wife and her newly found confidant discussed ways to bridge the gap between ethnic groups in the hospital waiting room, the partners in his firm were downtown in his office working frantically to minimize the impact of his absence.

The Brokerage Office of Gabrielle, Taylor & Phillips was one of the oldest and most successful in the Washington DC Area. The firm hired Alexander in 1987 when he graduated from the Harvard Business School. He was the most amazing non-white any of them had known personally. He was intelligent, highly motivated, and tough. Alexander knew the finance business inside and out and made huge amounts of money for the company. He climbed the corporate ladder to the top quicker than Jack Taylor, the senior partner, could remember anyone doing.

Lately, however, they all noticed a change in Alexander. He began questioning business decisions and the direction in which the firm was heading with considerable mention of social conscious, moral and ethical responsibility and other socio-political terms that successful financiers never wanted to hear uttered.

Taylor questioned the others for an explanation of Alexander's paradigm shift, but they had no answers. A colleague of Alexander's hired around the same time and who harbored resentment at Alexander's rapid climb within the corporation responded, "whatever his problem, this is a good time to get him the heck out of here! We've done our part for the great social experiment. This business," he exclaimed, "is about making money, its not about some darn left wing, bleeding heart, minority liberal, and his social welfare program!"

Alexander and his family were financially solid. They owned their home, had two cars and a dog, and Bianca attended a very good private school. But now, as he lay in a state of unconscious consciousness, his material world was being threatened. The threat was not just from the business partners who were the source of his income. There was also a heightened consciousness within him that was questioning his obsession with gaining wealth and status. He knew that wealth and status were not necessarily bad things in and of themselves, but when an individual sacrificed all of his morals and principles in order to gain material wealth, there emerges a moral and ethical dilemma.

8

"I can do all things through Him who strengthens me." (Phil 4:13)

Alexander knew the manboy who occupied his mind. He had been there many, many times before, but much more frequently as of late. Jimmy Lee Jenkins was a thirteen year old from Southeast, Washington DC. Alexander first met Jimmy Lee at the Brie Street Junior High School Business Fair. Alexander had volunteered to speak to the youngsters about careers in finance.

Jimmy Lee drew Alexander's attention because of the contrast between how this kid defined himself at this age and how Alexander remembered himself at the same age. Jimmy Lee was very pessimistic about his future and the future of those around him. He felt as though life had dealt him a terrible blow and he was destined to die in the streets before he reached twenty-one.

Jimmy Lee was nine years old when he had his first run in with the law. He was thirteen now and had not completed fifth grade. Jimmy Lee's parents were both crack heads who lived on the streets. There was no one to provide support for him, he hustled just to get food to eat.

Although they spoke only briefly, there was just enough time for Jimmy Lee to proclaim to Alexander that there was no reason for kids like him to listen to anything he had to say, because kids like him would never be given a chance to succeed in this society.

Jimmy Lee and the manboys of Washington forced Alexander to think back to Gas Bottom, a place he thought he had escaped. Jimmy Lee could have been a carbon copy of the young boys from Gas Bottom. Alexander imagined that Jimmy Lee might even look like his half brother whom he longed to see. He was always careful to search the eyes trying to imagine the tragic story that must accompany such a scraggly physical specimen. But he also scanned the eyes hoping to connect with one who might be his brother, the brother he never knew, the brother who probably felt that there was no hope for him to succeed either.

Jimmy Lee and all the manboys had become one. The manboy image was a double --edged sword that on the one hand revealed a devastatingly haunting image of the helplessness and hopelessness of a generation of young men, while on the other they represented the impotence of successful men such as Alexander who did little or not enough to help.

Even before the accident Alexander was concerned because he knew he wanted to and should do more. He needed to do much more than the occasional speech or talk at school, much more than the donations he made to charitable organizations. Alexander Rogers was a person whose spirit cried out for more than the body and mind was giving. He was an individual with strong moral convictions and a deep desire to help others. Alexander new that all that he had learned from his parents while growing up shaped and molded him into an individual who really cared about the plight of others. He needed to develop a plan to systematically identify and assist young men before they made the critical mistake that would handicap them for the rest of their life. He needed a plan to help his little brother and others like him who for whatever reason, were forced to grow up without a committed father pushing them towards excellence.

9

"What does the Lord require of you but to do justice, and to love kindness, and to walk humbly with your God?
(Mic 6:8)

Alexander's transformation began late one night in June after he and Alfre attended a jazz show at the Warner Theater in downtown DC. As they approached their vehicle after the show, they were startled to find a young man trying desperately to pry his way through the passenger side door. With a mason's brick that he found lying on the curb and with speed reminiscent of his glory days as an athlete, Alexander dashed toward the shadowy figure slamming him against the metallic green Mercedes that he was so proud to own. His second move, a slick half turn that he'd learned while wrestling in high school, brought the crook face down onto the dirty cement. In one cat --like motion, Alexander jerked the man's head around and raised the brick with a fury that he never knew before. He thought of his father and what it must have been like to be in a jungle where to kill or to be killed was the order of the day. At that split second, with beads of sweat forming on his forehead, and white pasty foam forming in the corners of his mouth, he stared deep into the eyes of the young human being he was perhaps about to kill. In an instant, he thought, everything that he had worked for would be gone. If he killed this young hoodlum who had the audacity to touch his beautiful, expensive Mercedes, it could destroy his entire family. He stopped! He squinted his eyes and tried to focus. His heart fluttered, his throat dry, he realized that the kid whose head he held in his trembling hands was the manboy Jimmy Lee Jenkins. He stopped abruptly, still holding the brick above his head, the boy slid from beneath him and scurried away, not knowing why he was spared, not really caring. He simply ran. He would live to see another day, that is all he lived for, anyway.

Alexander Rogers cried that night. He cried all night. He

cried for Jimmy Lee Jenkins, he cried for all the manboys of the world. He cried for his father and all the war veterans. He cried for his mother, and for all the mothers who had to raise manboys without their fathers. But most of all, he cried for himself. He cried because despite all of his personal successes; Harvard, his job, his home and cars, his family, he realized that he was not happy. Alexander understood at that moment that his uneasiness, the frustrations that he had experienced lately, the haunting image of Jimmy Lee Jenkins following him wherever he'd go, were all caused by his lack of action. Lying dormant within himself was a desire, an urge, a need to do something to help the manboys of the world.

Alexander's acknowledgment of his need led him to question his own values and the values of those around him. He began to feel that instead of concentrating so hard on oneself, he should make improving the lives of the not so fortunate our priority. We must realize that the manboys are human, they are worthwhile, and valuable, and without them, our society has a void. If these young men don't grow into productive adults, who will fill the void left by them? If the manboys of today are not taught to parent the children they father, what will happen to the next generation of manboys? Alexander was resigned to the notion that he would act. He would mount a change from within to do his part to help manboys experience a childhood of nurturing, guidance and understanding.

Alexander would begin his quest by urging men, including his father, to seek out and find their abandoned sons. Claiming one's own son and attempting to reconcile is a tremendous beginning, he thought. He would also educate men to the irreparable harm done by fathering children and not taking the responsibility to raise and care for them. He would emphasize that quality time spent with a young person is often much more valuable than money or other material things. He would say to friends and colleagues "if there is a young man in your immediate surroundings, your family, church, or neighborhood who does not have male supervision, then do all you can to provide a positive male presence in his life." Alexander hoped that one day he would find his brother. If he could find him, he would do everything in his power to turn the manboy's life around. He would insist that he pursue excellence as he did as a boy. He would demonstrate through his actions what a man ought to do.

Alexander Rogers understood the problem. Alexander had a plan. Alexander would execute his plan! When Alexander saw manboys on the street he would look at them differently. He would no longer assume that each teenager wearing baggy clothes, listening to hip-hop, is a menace to society. From this point forward when he look into the old, weary eyes of a manboy, he would search for a glimmer of hope. He would enlist friends and colleges alike to assist him in saving the manboys. He would tell everyone how easy it is to look through them, how easy it is to look past them, and how difficult it is to commit to helping them.

10

"Peace I leave with you; my peace I give to you. I do not give to you as the world gives. Do not let your hearts be troubled, and do not let them be afraid." (John 14:27)

As Dr. Brockington motioned for Nurse Chin to come into the room, Jimmy Lee Jenkins slowly lowered himself down and out of Alexander's consciousness, his mission complete. Alexander could feel himself regaining consciousness as the doctor explained his medical condition to his wife. Alexander slowly opened his eyes into the bright hospital light that hung loosely above his head. It reminded him of the bright light that fell upon him just as he was entering the Metro train. He squinted his eyes as his beautiful wife slowly came into focus. Thank God she was there! She was always there she would help him with his plan, together they would get things done. Standing near his spouse was a small person of Asian descent that he didn't recognize. Rose explained that the nurse had been with him since the accident and that he probably would not have made it without her. Rose calmly explained to Alexander the events of the day since his accident, and all that she and the nurse had gone through while he was unconscious. Alexander smiled through the bandages and thought to himself, whew! If they only knew what was happening on the inside!

11

"Jesus Christ is the same yesterday and today and forever."
(Heb 13:8)

When Alexander awoke from his long sleep in the forest he didn't know if what he remembered was real or a dream. His spirit renewed, his body and mind refreshed, he rose up and headed toward the city. The evening sun deflected a rainbow of colors off the dangling branches and leaves. The lighted rainbow marked the path that Alexander followed out of the woods and up the steep hill. The walk back through the city was different. He had a completely different perspective about getting things done. Helping the manboys was his challenge. He would work to provide for his family but he would work just as hard to fulfill his calling to help others. Alexander was hopeful instead of helpless. As he walked along he envisioned an oasis arising from the filth and rubble of the city. Manboys would be transformed into men with his help and the help of others like himself. He thought to himself: if every able man would stop and give a hand the transformation would not take nearly as long. Perhaps the toughest part of his job would be to convince others of the urgency of the situation, something that he had learned only after his unfortunate incident at the train station.

When Metro man arrived at his door there was no hesitation he sucked in his stomach and stuck his chest out as far as it would go, and rang the bell.

BAT NET

~1~

The blinking vacancy sign just outside the small, dusty, four paned window cast a strobe like shadow on the lanky figure lying across the motel bed. The man lay on his back, staring blankly at the floral design of the wallpaper plastered on the ceiling of the six-dollar per night room. The sparsely decorated room held a single wrought iron bed a four-drawer dresser and a lamp with a dusty shade covered in plastic.

Josh Stubblefield could feel the cold steel of the .32 caliber that lay on his chest. He felt the gun move up and down with each beat of his pounding heart. His index finger was wrapped firmly around the trigger housing, anticipating the moment when he would raise the barrel and fire at any intruder that entered the door.

Five days ago, Josh was an average law abiding citizen, managing, "Mega Bite," a computer sales and service store on Atlanta's South side. Tonight, his life turned completely upside down. He was chased out of his hometown by thugs, killed a man who was trying to kill him, and he still didn't have a clue as to what was going on. The most he knew was that he is held up in a cheap, dusty motel, wondering what his next move would be.

He couldn't shake the memory of the jagged edged dagger ripping the insides of his assailant as he yanked it out from his gut. He remembered the feel of the warm, sticky red blood as it gushed from the wound onto his arm. Most of all, Josh remembered the blank stare of the man with the weird tattoo inside his left ear as he slumped lifelessly against the back of the elevator. Josh never dreamed he could kill another human being yet in this instance he knew that it was either kill or be killed!

Josh stopped at a 7-11 over an hour ago to call his best friend Nate. The drive from Atlanta would take about forty minutes. He should be here by now. He smiled when he thought how easily Nate was distracted. Nate could very well be on his way to Oklahoma or some other strange place.

Nathaniel Means was older than Josh, but because they both had similar tastes and interests they hung out together. Nate was a semi-professional golfer a game he convinced Josh to take up a short time ago. They both were interested in computers; Josh, because of his business interests and Nate, as a hobby. Nate saw himself as a sort of homemade detective who could use computers and the Internet to develop his conspiracy theories. He'd actually gotten pretty good at conducting investigations and snooping into suspicious situations.

Suddenly!, there was a loud thumping on the door, followed by a rapid yellow gunfire that lit up the small room. Josh knew that the organization had come for him and that his small revolver was no match for the arsenal they were packing. He had one chance to escape. The narrow window hung over a slanted roof that sloped to the ground. If he could just make it to the window. Josh, remembering the three to five second rushes he learned in the Army, rolled off the bed just as a burst of machine gun fire tattooed the feathered mattress.

In a single bound, he was shattering the glass pane with his head as the door burst open and the two assassins went fully automatic towards the window. Josh landed on his butt and slid down the roof finally coming to rest on the hard concrete in front of the motel. At that moment, a black El Camino with chrome mud flaps screeched to a halt and out jumped Nate. "Sorry I'm late bro, but it seems as if I arrived just in time." He threw Josh into the open bed of the car and sped off. From his perch in the back of the car, Josh could see the two gangsters peering through the shattered upstairs window in disgust.

Nate gave the El Camino all the gas he could as the car sped through the dark streets of the small town. As they reached the highway, Josh tapped on the window and said, "Nate, I think I've been shot." You look okay to me where do you think you were shot? It feels like I was shot in the butt. Turn over demanded Nate as he examined the blood stained pants while continuing to drive at over 80 miles per hour. "That's just a piece of glass from the window stuck in your ass," exclaimed Nate with a silly smile. Nate instructed Josh to turn around and pull the glass from his butt and pour some vodka on it to sanitize it. Josh followed Nate's instructions and then took a swig from the half-empty vodka bottle. The stinging pain subsided as the warm vodka made its way through his system. Josh began to feel better. He felt better because he escaped without being shot and he was with his buddy Nate.

2

Josh pushed the sliding window open, climbed through the front and gingerly took his seat beside Nate. Josh began to explain to Nate how he ended up at the motel. Josh recalled how his video security camera at the computer store picked up two huge men in dark suits and sunglasses forcing their way into a back door at the loading dock. They each carried oozies with silencers. The close-up of the men showed tattoos in their left ear's. Josh thought the tattoo looked like a bat with its wings spread. Nate started to speak, but allowed Josh to continue. Josh went on. "I dropped everything and slipped out the front door. I ran to my car as fast as these feet would take me. Once I entered the parking garage and was approaching my car, I heard the squealing wheels of a speeding automobile coming up the ramp. I darted into the stairwell just as a car with what looked like the two men who had broken into the store sped past. I ran up the stairs to the top of the garage. Through a stroke of luck, a tow truck was hooking up a disabled car and I was able to escape because the hoods didn't want to be spotted taking me out. I made it to the Greyhound station and took the first outbound bus. I checked into the motel and then called you." Josh, "do you have any idea of what we have gotten into, asked Nate?" Josh looking dumb and scared softly stated "no, but I'm sure you are about to tell me." Nate checked his rear view mirror to see if anyone was following, and then, pulled over onto the shoulder of the road. After relieving himself he hopped back into the car and sped off. Nate began to speak. The tattoo you saw on the close-up was a bat. The bat is the symbol worn by the members of a notorious white-collar gang that the feds have been after for years. BATNET, as they refer to themselves, is a hand full of med-to-large sized computer data companies with no legal acknowledged association. Their leader is Martin Abercrombie, a brilliant ex-con who did three years at the federal center for electronic stock fraud. Abercrombie was a communications genius who decided that there was much more money to be made illegally than on the stock market. With his billions and boyish charisma, he convinced other businessmen to connect to his invisible data net, which intercepted electronic funds from large international financial institutions. Abercrombie and his web of data pirates would intercept huge electronic money transfers from companies with ties to illegal activity. The cleverly designed interception would re-direct multi-million dollar transfers to Swiss accounts controlled by BATNET. The unsuspecting companies would then be contacted through an electronic message that would override their computer system and appear on the monitor. The CEO of the hijacked company would be told of BATNET's knowledge of his company's illegal ties and activities and that he should simply forget the transfer and send another payment. If the CEO refused, BATNET would make sure that the right people received word of the illegal activities of the company. The amount of money lost on this hijacked transaction pales to the losses that would be associated with a tarnished reputation and possible criminal charges." Nate went on barely taking a breath. "BATNET's electronic data component is manned by a large army of military styled strongmen, whose job is to enforce the will of the organization. This group of hit men and assassins are deadly. Each wears a tattoo inside the left ear. It's a tattoo of a bat, with wings fully spread, that symbolizes the organization's ability to trap it's prey." Josh interrupted, "that's a little cocky isn't it?" "Cocky is not the word" added Nate. "These bastards strut their stuff like they are one of the Fortune 500 companies. They don't believe they can be stopped." Josh added, "from where I'm sitting I'd say they are just about right."

Josh, feeling tired and worn from a day of chaos, and the non-stop talking of his friend recalled how he and Nate first stumbled on to this scheme. While hacking on a brand new, high-powered computer they noticed that a local financial institution sent two, half-million dollar payments to the same company with the same invoice number. The situation became more curious when Nate, acting in his role as private investigator, decided to call a company employee to see if they were aware of the mistake. The employee abruptly ended the conversation and hung up the phone. Minutes later, all evidence of the first transaction was gone from their computer, as though it never existed.

These strange events wet the appetite of the would-be investigator and his friend the computer storeowner. They began hacking on a regular basis trying to make sense out of what they'd stumbled upon.

3

Instead of driving back to Atlanta, Nate turned off onto a country road about twenty miles outside of the 285 perimeter. "Where are we going Nate?" Josh asked curiously as he awakened from a quick nap. "There's someone I want you to meet. Someone who I think can help us and indeed may save our lives."

About five miles off the main road, they came upon a tremendous iron gate, purposefully over-run by cutzu and other vegetation. Nate spoke into the voice box from his rolled down window and the big iron gate rose just enough to let the top of the vehicle pass through. Josh was not prepared for what happened next. The car was on a platform just inside the gate when it began to descend slowly beneath the surface. After what seemed like 10 minutes, though it was actually 2.3 minutes, the moving platform stopped. Another gate opened and they rolled out into a huge enclave of satellite dishes, computers, and what looked like thousands of other electronic devices, each with green and red flickering lights. Josh was speechless. His mouth hanging open, his eyes as wide as silver dollars. Nate was excited also but less so than Josh because he had apparently visited this place before. A loud but pleasant voice filtered out through the intercom, "it's okay to dismount gentleman."

Nate leaped from the car like a kid entering a game room at the mall, while Josh followed slowly. "Can you believe this?" asked Nate. "What the hell have you gotten us into?", Josh asked in a subdued voice as if he didn't have enough oxygen remaining to get the last word out. Before Nate had a chance to answer a tall, slender, intelligent looking man with wire framed glasses and a radio transmitter around his head, approached with an outstretched hand. He and Nate shook hands vigorously like old friends. The two then turned to Josh. "Josh this is Dr. Felipi Von Brie." Josh asked sarcastically, "are you real or are you a cyborg?" The two chuckled and Josh seemed to loosen up a bit. The doctor explained that his place was the largest of four

Electro Data Surveillance Sites (EDSS) in the continental United States. "Yeah, yeah" shouted Josh impatiently, "but what does that have to do with us?" "Let me continue" said the doctor. "Our mission is to ensure the security of all electronic data links that transmit from or into the country." Come with me, motioned the doctor. The three men strolled over to a huge computer terminal with a life size monitor. Dr. Von Brie touched a couple of buttons and what appeared on the screen nearly caused Josh to faint. There it was in black and white across the monitor. That tattoo that he'd seen on the man who tried to kill him. It was the BATNET emblem.

"What the heck is it?", asked Josh. "You are looking at the trademark of one of the largest and most vicious data pirating organizations in the world. They call themselves BATNET. We estimate they have bilked financial institutions out of hundreds of millions of dollars over the last five years."

"So we were right!" shouted Nate exuberantly. "What we uncovered in Atlanta was evidence that SSS Financial bank made a second payment to a customer because the first one was intercepted by BATNET." "Yeah, and that little discovery nearly caused me my life!" said Josh. "So tell me Dr. Von Brie, if you know all of this, why haven't you stopped them?" "They are a very careful organization. "We have no hard evidence that will stand up in court. Each time we think we have a witness, he ends up missing or dead."

"Okay Nate, lets get the hell out of here right now because you know I don't have any insurance, and I don't want my body lying around for weeks while the local churches collect enough money for my burial." "I'm afraid it's too late," explained a solemn Dr. Von Brie. "They tracked your activity to your computer store and they won't stop until they eliminate you both." "I knew all of this computer and detective stuff would eventually get us into trouble. My mother even told me "boy, you better stop messing around with them there electric boxes before they electrocute you!" Well, we may not get electrocuted, but when the BATNET finishes with us, we'll wish we had been," Josh exclaimed.

Von Brie removed his glasses in deep contemplation and said, "we have one chance to stop them. The authorities have everything in place ready to move in on these guys but we need your testimony pertaining to the evidence you uncovered in your computer store." "Wait a minute Doc! I know we've known each other for a long time and I even owe you a couple of favors, but I never expected you'd ask me to risk my life when you called last week." "Gentlemen, this is much bigger and far more important than you could ever imagine."

4

Josh and Nate made it back to the outside of the complex without speaking. It was hard for either of them to comprehend the magnitude of it all, but they knew their lives would never be the same. Josh spoke first. "All I ever wanted to do was to own my own business make a little money and live happily ever after. Now, here I am a simple guy, in the middle of the biggest electronic fraud shit in the history of the universe." "I know" said Nate, "being a small time private detective is one thing, but this is ridiculous. Okay, you know what we've got to do. We'll meet back at the store at 0600, BATNET will never think that we'd be stupid enough to go back there again." Josh spoke up, "I'll prepare the dummies and leave them in the car. God, I hope Von Brie's plan works." Nate said resolutely, "if it doesn't, we will cease to exist."

Von Brie had outlined in detail every move the two would make for the next 24 hours. They would go back to the store and log on to the Internet. BATNET's reconnaissance would detect them almost instantaneously. Yet, the two heroes would have to remain in the store while the gangsters booby-trapped their car. While in the store and logged on to the Internet, they reminisced about old times. The two men realized how fond they were of each other and how they had covered for each other hundreds of times. It was an unusual conversation, one that men didn't feel comfortable having. But for Nate and Josh it seemed the most natural thing to do considering the precarious predicament they found themselves in.

"Who would have thought?", asked Nate. "After today we will never lay eyes on or talk to each other again." "Yeah," agreed Josh "and all because of some frigging bats. But you know what? I'm glad we uncovered their dirty secret. Poor people are always getting busted for crimes, nickel and dime crimes. Yet they get most of the long sentences. Remember the guy who got five years for stealing a loaf of bread and a can of beans?" "Hell yeah I remember that. I remember it well because two years later the accountant for the parent corporation for that same store was given community service and probation embezzling 3 million dollars. Yeah, I'm glad we are bringing these bastards down. We are doing it for the little people."

Nate and Josh were prepared to move out at 0655. Von Brie had assured them that the booby trap would be in place by then. The two heroes hugged each other, said their Hail Mary's and walked calmly out of the door. They did not look at each other, they did not speak. They knew both friend and foe were watching them. And, as a matter of fact they weren't really sure if BATNET and Von Brie or both were the enemy. Exactly ten seconds after Josh closed the passenger side door, the air was filled with a gigantic fireball.

The fire department extinguished what was left of the charred wreckage and SGT Malloy, a special officer with the Von Brie connection roped off the area. No one, was to enter the area except the coroner. The coroner, another agent of Von Brie's, arrived twenty minutes later and pronounced that Josh Stubblefield and Nate Pierson died at 0705 from the explosion and the fire.

The newspapers called it a tragedy and reported that a freak gas tank explosion killed the two entrepreneurs. EDSS and Dr. Von Brie were able to tape record the order to kill given by Gilbert Abercrombe when he was notified that Nate and Josh had returned to their store. The tape also captured Abercrombie and his inner circle discussing plans to blackmail other companies. It was all the Federal Prosecutors would need to bust the multi-billion dollar electronic Mafia.

5

It was a cool rainy day. The white blinking lights of the Space Needle created a strobe like effect on the shadowy figure as he sat on the park bench starring aimlessly at passersby. He arrived in Seattle exactly one week ago with no luggage, no past, just memories. Memories of his last days in Atlanta played over and over in his head like a vinyl album with a scratch on it. He remembered sliding down through the hole in the floor of the El Caiman and into the open manhole. The manhole cover was barely in place when the explosion rang out in his ears and the heat seared the hair from his arms and hand. The trip through the sewer, and down to the river would remain with him as long as he lived. The last time he saw his friend, his only connection to his other life, was when he ducked into the helicopter and sped off. He wondered, each day, where he ended up.

As he limped back to his studio apartment, his hands bandaged in sterile white gauze, Charlie Yates trembled violently for several seconds as a haunting thought forced its way into his brain: "Maybe I ought and buy myself a computer!"

MANO Y MANO

(A not so serious look at man looking at himself.)

Introduction

Just look at us sitting here wide-eyed, mis-represented and often misunderstood, Man that is. In this era of psycho-analysts, psychotics, and psychic hotlines you would think someone would take the time and thoroughly analyze the male of the human species and his actions. M-a-n, put the man in mankind and is the source of one of the most thought provoking questions of our day: "who's da man?" On the pages that follow I will attempt to uncover, (No this is not "X" rated)some of the inner thoughts of "man" so that the world might begin to understand him better.

I think you all will agree that there is an awful lot of literature on the physically weaker, the esthetically more beautiful, the inherently more wiser of the human species, woman! Writers and soothsayers alike have all but exhausted their investigation of the physical woman and all of her wonders, the emotional woman and all of her moods, and the working woman and her innate drive to take care of her family. One, however, is hard pressed to find any works, scholarly or otherwise on who "man" really is and what makes him tick, or for that matter, what ticks him off. This essay, then, is an attempt to give "man" his due. Let's look at him through his own eye, Mano Y Mano!

The intent of this essay is to allow man to look at himself, make observations about himself and to move on or indeed to stand still where he is. If you are reading this story from the perspective of anyone other than man, please do not assume that I intend any harm or ill feelings towards you. In this case I am simply poking fun while identifying and probing the thoughts of man.

Each section of the essay represents an area that deserves more attention because of the unique perspective man has on the particular subject. You will find, hopefully, some underlying moral truths, food for thought, and arrows that point us from darkness towards light, and lastly, quite a bit of bull. So, if you are ready for a journey into the inner mechanisms of man's thought processes go ahead, turn the page!

~1~

Man on Man

No, this is not another sports term. Why are men painted so broadly as pathetic slaves to sport? We are so much deeper than that. Man on man in this particular instance addresses the notion that men should begin to define and discuss who they are amongst themselves. Lets face it, what or who a man is differs across a thousand lines. There are, cultural, religious, political, ethnic, hemispheric, shoe size, amount of hair, blue collar, white collar, no collar, cheese-eating, non-cheese eating, fat, skinny, smart, stupid, cockiness, cocklessness, and many many more ways for man to differ. But despite or through it all, a man is a man. (*All men beat your chest with your fist a couple of times*!) Come on, do it one time for the boys. Beat that damn chest and make some kind of crazy noise. Do it because you are man!

Despite all of our differences, we recognize manliness in other men. Hell no we don't go around shouting "now there's real man" or high fiving strangers or any other ridiculous shenanigans but inside, we humbly acknowledge manhood in other men. Sadaam, despite all of his rhetoric, quietly acknowledges that Bill is a man and has to do the job he thinks he has to do, just like he does. Man's ability to acknowledge other men, perhaps, contributes to man's ability to strategize against his enemies: because we all know that a man has to do what a man has to do!

Every man knows every man. When a woman complains about something a man did or didn't do, to her or for her, every other man knows that she is probably pretty close to being right. It's simply a matter that each of us knows that the man in question is capable and likely to be guilty. If her man is guilty all men are implicated. For example, your neighbor comes over and is talking with you and your wife and she says:' that damn Roger ain't worth a shit. Wherever he takes off a piece of clothing he leaves it. He won't let the toilet seat down when he

79

finishes and he still pees all over the toilet! All we can do at that point is nod our heads and think to ourselves, "What's so wrong with any of that?"

When men come in contact with, confront, meet, see, or think of other men, size and stature always come into play. I believe there is a prototype male physique. While we give our female sisters all the credit, men are just as guilty of sizing each other up. We think, am I taller than he is, am I stronger, how would he look with my hair, how would I look with his muscles, how in the hell did he get built like that, how did I turn out this short and round? But, in the end, when comparisons are all done, we walk away with what we have and rationalize that it ain't too bad. Maybe women could learn a lesson from us.

While men do not love as hard as women, they can hate as hard. Men who hate will kill because the hate in them is greater than the love of self. Young men who kill, kill because they hate themselves, and their situation. They hate everything, so they kill. If older, smarter, bigger more loving men could reduce the hate in those young men, it would help resolve some of the problems of our young men today. Hate is like a cancer. It grows and eventually consumes. Men need to recognize that there is a cure for hate: it's love. We need to learn to tell other men that love is good, and it's all right for us to love. We men, have a capacity to love equal to that of women. If we look back at our lives, our family, we can see situations where we could have shown love but instead we showed something else. When we are hurt, we turn to hate. Hate is our revenge for hurt. Wouldn't it be great if men could look each other in the eye and say, "let go of the hate." I believe it's hate that makes us join irrational groups. We have a hatred inside and when we find a group that exposes hate, it's easy for us to identify with that group. Imagine this, a man in each hate group realizes that he can overcome his hate and live a much freer life. He then begins to tell each member, "Let go of the hate." And as the hate relinquishes, love moves in, the destructive forces subside, the cancer goes into remission. Now wouldn't that be something? When we empty our plate of hate, we begin to fill our cup with love. Men, we are the only ones who can do it. We are the purveyors of hate and all bad things associated with it. We can make things better, we can fix it. It's in our hands. Women can't help because they don't understand the depth of the hate because our capacity to hate runs so much deeper than theirs.

Finally men, there is a disgusting phenomenon that we need to come to grips with. All of the world outside of us (women, children, and others) feel that we are engaged in a conspiracy to pollute the air with foul smells and sonic booms. That's right, we're accused of malicious farting. Not just farting to allow pent up gas to escape, but farting to make ourselves happy and to make others suffer. Is any of this true?

Can any of you nice mannerable guys reading these pages call up an egg smelling fart right now? Yes, some of you could, and you'd be quite pleased with yourselves if you did. How do we do it? Is there something about the male's physiological make up that makes him more susceptible to farting? Or, is it a mental thing? When our grandparents call little boys "stinker" are they inadvertently creating a psychological condition that causes males to fart uncontrollably all of their lives? I don't know the answer but something sure smells funny. As if farting is not enough, the majority of us men have engaged others in the sport of farting by having people pull our finger. How many of you guys have done that? Good, now you're admitting it, all of you! Next will come the healing.

We've really got to move on from here. Just remember, we are all fart-o-holics. Just one fart away from going into a fart loop that will send us spinning out of control around the world. Boy, what a hole that would put in the ozone layer.

Men really love sports, it's hard to explain why. I mean, if you take the point of view that men like sports because it gets him away from his nagging woman for prolonged periods of time, then you would have to agree that this is a recent phenomenon. Since sports have become the main stay of television, perhaps some men have used sports as a vehicle to free them from the delightfully peaceful and serene company of their female partner. But what about the time before television was invented?

There is obviously a connection between testosterone or balls (can we call them balls?), and sports. I recall a story by a doctor trying to deliver a stubborn baby who just didn't seem to want to come out. The mother in her anxiety sighed, "Oh he's just a stubborn boy." The doctor's eyes became as wide as half-dollars. You know, like a quarterback's eyes when you see him under center. The doctor shouted, hut one, hut two, hike! The eight-pound baby popped out like the cork on a bottle of champagne. So you see: men are into sports even before they leave the womb, so deal with it.

Speaking of beer. I know I didn't mention beer but is there any greater marriage in the universe than beer and sports? I'm sure you readers are thirsty for a beer right now just because we are talking about sports. It's natural. Beer and sports go together just like smoking and going to the bathroom. When we watch sports we want beer. Why do you think most beer commercials involve some aspect of sports? Our concerned female readers are probably asking, "How can you knuckleheads enjoy the game when you drink so much beer?" We can't! We are just too wrapped up in this sports phenomenon to admit it. There are many lies told when discussing sports. Because of the beer, men don't really remember what happened in a game so they just speculate. We read the sports section of the newspaper first each morning so that if someone comes up to us with some conversation about a game or an athlete we can respond on the spot with some bullshit that we just read in the paper.

Playing sports, watching sports, and talking about sports is lots of fun. Ladies, you can really capitalize on man's love for sport. If you want to try to capture a guy, just act like you are into sports, or better yet, get into sports! Guys admit it we are suckers for women who like sports.

2

Man on Women

Men and women are totally different creatures, Duh! We can look at the exact same object and see totally different things. As mentioned in the introduction, scholars, social scientist, psychologists, etc. have examined women inside and out to the point of exhaustion. But rarely, if ever, do we have a chance to see what the common man has to say about women. Sure, some of the stuff written about women has come from men, but not the common man. Perhaps the reason is: nobody wants to hear what men have to say about women. Well, what do you know, here is your opportunity. Let's talk about women.

They talk too much. Women talk too damn much. Whether it's in the bed after sex, on the telephone, in the car, in church, it does not matter, women simply talk too much. We are not mad at them for talking are we? No, just a little annoyed. Why is it that when the news anchor is just about to explain the breaking news story, or when your team is going in for the winning touchdown in overtime, women want to talk. We love you dearly but could you please cut down on your oral dissertations. Men talk, but we talk a lot of bullshit. Right guys! Women, you are much too serious in the topics you want to discuss. Men do not want to talk about what they would do if their wife died and left them with the children! That's too deep. Let's talk about who is going to win the Stanley Cup next year. That's interesting stuff. Men don't want to talk about anything that will end up making them cry. And that's all women want to talk about.

Let's talk about sex. It seems that men always want to have or to talk about sex. Now, what we really believe is that women want it and want to talk about it as much as men do. However, women don't talk about it in order to make men look like nymphomaniacs. Despite the fact that women don't want to talk about it or do it, when they do have sex they always want the

83

man to do it longer than he does it! What's that all about? Are women trying to shame us into doing it less by pretending that we really can't give it to them as long as they would like it? Now that's hitting below the belt!

Men really like the way women smell. I don't think women know the depth of this basic animal instinct. Because I'm trying to keep the book's content rated "PG", I can't really go into detail on this smell thing. But ladies, you could really get a lot more mileage by manipulating us with your array of smells. Why do you suppose the male species of most animals always approach the female with his nose?

More on love. Men really love their women much, much more than they will ever say. We are apparently handicapped by nature and simply unable to express our love the way we could and should. We just wish there was a way for women to look down deep into us and to see the love that we have for them. It's kind of like that great sneeze that just won't come out. You know it's there, you know it will feel good if you get it out, but it just won't come out. Women, you are right about one thing, we always miss you when you're gone. We never want you to leave but we are too manly and stupid to tell you not to go. If you love us, chances are we love you too. That's just the way love goes. Even the man who makes his woman walk one step behind him, loves her dearly. We need you, we want you, we love you.

Men, we need to help each other understand how much our women really want us to show our love. One way we can help each other is to take every opportunity to show other men that you are not afraid to express your love for your woman. No, that does not make you a punk, it just makes you a little sensitive.

Do women like, want, or need variety to a tremendously less degree than men? Why is it always the man who is getting scolded for wandering off, trying new and different versions of things? I think this is a legitimate question. The answer lies in the statement made at the beginning of this section: women and men are totally different creatures. Wait, that's over simplification isn't it? A woman's eye may wander as much as a man's, but a woman isn't as easily pulled to another man because she has expressed her love more freely and openly than her male partner. The freedom that a man will gain by openly and consistently expressing his love for his woman may be enough to offset his innate desire to continuously move from pasture to pasture. Hey guys, its worth a shot.

Guys, how do you feel about women drinking from your drink or eating from your food? I'll tell you how I feel! STOP IT! You see, it would be okay if about once a year your woman would say oh honey that looks good may I taste it? Or if every now and then she'd say, that looks really refreshing, may I have a sip? Unfortunately that's not the way it generally happens. Women seem to make a habit of refusing food or drink for themselves and immediately partaking of her male partner's stuff. WE don't like that. As a matter of fact we hate it. Women, why don't you just get some for your self? Its not cute its not romantic, its simply annoying. There now, do you understand how man feels about that.

3

Man, Woman and Power

Our primary struggle has always been about power. Since Eve used her powers to persuade Adam to do something he knew he shouldn't do the question has been who has the power.

There seems to be some discrepancy over who should be the leader in a relationship and if in fact leadership is related to gender.   Movements by women's groups seem to have established in the minds of many women that is bad for them to allow the male to serve in the leadership role in a heterosexual relationship. Men feel that women are stupid for trying to control things in a relationship. A relationship like a team, a business or any other group is best run by one leader.   It is helpful to have one leader because things work smoother that way. Man perhaps is the natural leader although the issue can be debated to infinity.   There are lots of assumption necessary in order to accept this point of view. Man is physically stronger and braver in the face of danger. If this is true it does make sense for man to be the leader in a male/female relationships although obviously there is much more to leadership. We gladly accept the role of leader but we all fear that one day our women will scold us for being too over powering or domineering. Ladies let the man lead. Someone has to play the role of leader in a relationship. If your man is willing and capable let him lead. Well, ladies, there is not much worse then having your leadership challenged by your woman.

4

Raising Boys

I am not sure if it's harder to raise boys or girls but I am sure that it's different. There is quite a bit of discussion these days on whether single parent families headed by females can do an adequate job of parenting male children. An alarming percentage of families in minority communities are lead by women. It's obvious that the reason there are so many families in this predicament is that the mother and father of the children are not together.

Now, Man to Man let's talk about why men leave their children. The issue is complicated by the fact that whenever a man leaves his family he is most often leaving his female companion. The consequence of such action is that children are left without a father.

Sometimes, make that lots of times, I think we leave too soon. I am not saying that there aren't compelling reasons to leave but I am saying there are more compelling reasons to stay. Do you know how hard it is for a young man to grow up? Of course you do you were once a young man yourself. Boys need men close by to observe and to pattern their behaviors. If you argue some boys with fathers and male role models end up having problems then you will get no argument from me. However, overall, I think we can all agree that boys that grow up in a home where their father or male figure is present will have a better chance to succeed. Some of you have turned out to be perfect men without your fathers and I commend you, everyone is not as lucky.

I applaud all of the strong, loving, resourceful women out there who must raise their children alone. A great deal of you are in your current predicament because your man left you with the children. Shame on us. Some of you are in your current predicament because you left your man. There are situations that women face that leave them no choice but to bail out. But like I mentioned earlier, just like some men, some of you leave too soon. You leave perhaps without considering the consequences to your children.

Boys need men to learn manly stuff from. Yes, women give boys a tremendous amount of love and nurturing but like my homeboy stated so eloquently: "A woman can't teach a boy how to pee."

This situation is critical because so many boys are lost to homicide, jail and drugs. Some things are way beyond our control. Whether we stay at home and raise our boys or flee to other partners is our choice.

Conclusion

The feelings and emotions of man span the entire spectrum. They are not confined to aggression, lustfulness and confrontation. My contention is that there is not nearly enough concern and or investigation into his true feelings. This essay has explored how men really feel about certain aspects of life where little concern was expressed in the past.

If you laughed even once while reading this piece my mission is successful. The intent was to make you laugh and at the same time offer you some thoughts to ponder.

Good night.

The End

About The Author

Dr. Arthur P. McMahan was born in Spartanburg, SC where he attended public school. He attended the University of South Carolina before beginning his distinguish career as an US Army Officer. He received a Doctor of Philosophy degree from VA Commonwealth University in 1996. Dr. McMahan is currently working on his second book which is scheduled to be completed in 2000.

Breinigsville, PA USA
27 February 2011
256435BV00001B/7/A

9 781587 213755